The Case of the Zoo Clue

to
Amberley

Look for these Clue™ Jr. books!

Clue Jr.

The Case of the Zoo Clue

Book created by Parker C. Hinter

Written by Della Rowland

Illustrated by Chuck Slack

Based on characters from the Parker Brothers game

A Creative Media Applications Production

SCHOLASTIC INC.
New York Toronto London Auckland Sydney

ISBN 0-590-62372-9

Copyright © 1996 by Waddingtons Games Ltd. All rights reserved. Published by Scholastic Inc. by arrangement with Parker Brothers, a division of Tonka Corporation. CLUE® is a registered trademark of Waddingtons Games Ltd. for its detective game equipment.

22 21 20 19 18 17 16 15 14   1/0

Printed in the U.S.A.   40

First Scholastic printing, February 1996

Contents

Introduction

Meet the members of the Clue Club.

Samantha Scarlet, Peter Plum, Georgie Green, Wendy White, Mortimer Mustard, and Polly Peacock.

These young detectives are all in the same fourth-grade class. The thing they have most in common, though, is their love of mysteries. They formed the Clue Club to talk about mystery books they have read, mystery TV shows and movies they like to watch, and also, to play their favorite game, Clue Jr.

These mystery fans are pretty sharp when it comes to solving real-life mysteries, too. They all use their wits and deductive skills to crack the cases in this book.

You can match *your* wits with this gang of junior detectives to solve the eight mysteries. Can you guess who did it? Check the solution that appears upside down after each story to see if you were right!

The Case of the Zoo Clue

Briiinnng! The school bell blared out across the school yard. Everyone started to walk toward the school doors, except the Clue Club kids and the rest of their fourth-grade class.

"This is a great way to start the school day," Georgie Green said to Peter Plum. "Not going to school."

"I don't mind school," Peter said. "Actually, I really like it."

"Well, today we all like school," said Mortimer Mustard, "because we'll be at the zoo instead."

One of the giraffes at the Hobart Natural Zoo had just given birth, and Ms. Redding decided to take her fourth-grade class to see the new baby. She told the class that they would see a slide show on giraffes

3

first. "After the slide show, we'll go look at the baby giraffe," she explained. "Then we'll walk around and look at some of the other animals." The Clue kids cheered. "All right," Ms. Redding said, "let's get on the bus. And don't run!"

The Clue Club hurried to the back of the bus so they could sit together. Georgie and Peter took the second-to-last seat, while Mortimer, Wendy White, Samantha Scarlet, and Polly Peacock slid into the back row.

As soon as the driver started up the engine, Peter said, "I know we're having a slide show, but I did some reading myself on giraffes last night."

"Oh, no," Wendy said. "That means he's going to give us a lecture."

Peter ignored Wendy. "Giraffes are the tallest animals in the world," he began.

"Duh, Peter," said Polly. "Even we know that."

"Well, did you know the new baby we're

4

going to see was six feet tall when it was born?" Peter asked.

"I didn't!" exclaimed Samantha. "That's tall!"

"That's how long a full-grown giraffe's neck is, too," Peter went on. "Six feet."

"Wow," said Mortimer. "A six-foot neck. It must take a long time for the giraffe's food to get down to its stomach. It would still be hungry, even after it ate. Which reminds me, I packed a snack for the ride."

"Here's a question about giraffes for you guys," Peter said. "How many bones are in a giraffe's neck — seven, thirteen, or twenty?"

"If its neck is six feet long, it would need at least twenty bones," said Georgie.

"Wrong," said Wendy. "They have the same number as we do. Seven."

"No way!" exclaimed Georgie.

"That's right," said Peter. "But of course the bones are much bigger than ours. They have to be. They have to support a five-hundred-and-fifty-pound neck. But even with that huge neck, giraffes make almost no noise. Sometimes they moan or snort, but not very often. And you can hardly hear it when they do."

"Okay," said Polly. "But Ms. Redding said giraffes warn other animals when enemies are coming. How do they do that if they don't make any noise?"

"I know the answer to this one, Peter," Wendy said. "A lot of animals hang around giraffes for safety. Giraffes are so tall they can see a dangerous animal from far off. If they see a lion coming toward them, they run for a safe place. That's the clue for the other animals to be on the lookout."

"Oh," said Polly.

"Giraffes are like living watchtowers," giggled Georgie.

Just then the bus drove through the entrance to the zoo. "Here we are, class," said Ms. Redding. "Everyone line up outside the bus."

Mrs. Mead, the tour guide, led the class

into the viewing room to watch the slide show. When Mrs. Mead asked if anyone knew how many bones were in a giraffe's neck, Georgie jumped out of his chair. "Seven," he answered proudly. "The same as ours."

"Very good, Georgie," said Ms. Redding, a little surprised. The Clue Club looked at each other and smiled.

After the slide show, everyone headed out to the field where the giraffes were kept. The tall animals were grouped together around the new baby.

"Wow!" exclaimed Samantha when she saw the baby giraffe. "They really *are* tall! The baby looks taller than my dad!"

"Imagine having a pet giraffe," said Mortimer.

"It couldn't curl up at the foot of my bed like my dog Bizzy likes to do," said Peter.

Mrs. Mead pointed out the giraffe's food. "You can see that the giraffes' feeding troughs are very high up," she told the class. "As you just learned, we do that so the giraffes don't have to bend down to the ground to eat. With their long legs and neck, that's very difficult for them. We even put their drinking water up high."

"I read that the giraffe's heart weighs twenty-five pounds," Peter said. "It's bigger than usual so that it can pump blood all the way up the neck. It can pump a bathtub full of blood every three minutes."

"Yuk!" cried Polly. "Thanks for sharing that, Peter."

"Well, let's go on to the birdhouse," said Ms. Redding. The class followed Mrs. Mead to the birdhouse. It was a beautiful tall building made entirely of glass.

"Look at all the parrots!" said Wendy. The brightly colored birds made her think of her own pet parrot. "Petunia would like to visit here."

"She might see some of her relatives," laughed Georgie.

"Next we're going to the big cat pavilion," Mrs. Mead told the children as they left the birdhouse. "I'm afraid we don't have any tigers because they are endangered. The few that are left in the wild are on game preserves in Asia."

Just then everyone heard yelling coming from the bottom of the hill. They all turned to look. They saw Bill Black and Greg Greyford fighting in front of the fence.

Ms. Redding ran to the boys, with Mrs. Mead and the class behind her. "Boys! Boys! Stop that this instant," she cried. "What do you think you're doing?"

"Bill was throwing rocks at the giraffes!" shouted Greg. "I told him I was going to tell and he started hitting me."

"He's a liar!" screamed Bill. "He's the one who threw the rocks! He's just trying to get out of it."

"Wait, wait, wait!" said Ms. Redding. "Everyone settle down. Start from the beginning. Bill, you first."

"Well, I was behind the feeding bins watching the giraffes eat, when everyone left for the birdhouse," said Bill. "When I came around the corner I saw Greg throw-

ing rocks at the baby giraffe. I couldn't believe it! I told him to quit but he just laughed. Then I said I was going to tell. That's when he started hitting me. I had to fight back."

"You big liar!" shouted Greg.

"All right, Greg, calm down," said Ms. Redding. "Now you tell me your side."

"Everything's the way he told it," said Greg. "Except it was me behind the feeding stalls. I was almost to the birdhouse when I heard the giraffes whining. I turned around and saw he was throwing rocks at them. I ran back to make him stop, and that's when you saw us."

"Well, one of you is lying," said Ms. Redding. "And we're not going anywhere until we hear the truth."

"I just heard the truth," said Polly. "And it didn't come from you, Greg."

How does Polly know Greg is lying?

Solution
The Case of the Zoo Clue

"How do you know what happened, Polly?" cried Greg. "You weren't even here."

"I wasn't *here*, but I know what you didn't *hear*," Polly said. "And I know you didn't *hear* the giraffe."

"That's right," said Mortimer. "Giraffes rarely make a sound, and when they do, it's very soft."

"So even if the giraffes made a noise, there's no way you could have heard it from the birdhouse," Polly continued. "You made up your story to throw the blame on Bill."

"You should be ashamed, Greg," said Ms. Redding. "Throwing rocks at these gentle creatures. You can just sit in the bus until we've finished in the zoo."

"Looks like Greg was hearing things when he came up with that story," said Georgie.

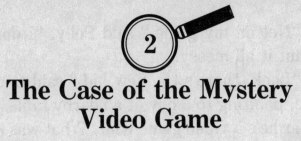

The Case of the Mystery Video Game

"Lunch is my favorite class period," sighed Mortimer Mustard as he took a second tuna sandwich from his lunch bag.

The Clue Club kids were trying to decide if they had time for a game of Clue Jr. before the bell rang.

"I'm finished eating," said Polly Peacock. "How about the rest of you?"

"Me, too," said Peter Plum.

"Me, three," chimed in Wendy White.

"Wanna swap my cupcake for your fruit bar?" Georgie Green asked Samantha Scarlet.

"Okay," said Samantha.

"I still have some peanut butter crackers and an apple left," said Mortimer. "But I can eat and play Clue Jr."

"Not on my game," said Polly. "I don't want it all messy."

"Look, there's the new kid," said Georgie, pointing to a boy at a nearby table. "I hear he's a video game whiz. What was his name?"

"Don't point," cried Polly. "Didn't your parents teach you any manners? And his name is Paul Pearly."

"Hey, Paul," called Peter. "Come here!"

Paul walked over to sit with the Clue kids. "Hi," Paul said.

"Hi," Mortimer said while sticking the last half of his sandwich in his mouth.

"Where do you live?" Samantha asked Paul.

"Over on Redwood Street," he replied. "It's the gray brick house across from the candy store."

"That's near my house," said Wendy. "We're neighbors."

"Speaking of candy," said Mortimer. "I thought I had one more thing for lunch."

He pulled a chocolate bar from his lunch bag.

"Umm," sighed Polly. "Chocolate is my favorite candy. What's yours, Paul?"

"I can't eat candy or sugar," said Paul. "I'm diabetic."

"Can't eat candy?" said Georgie. "Wow, that's awful."

"It doesn't really bother me," said Paul. "Only around Halloween, I guess. But my folks usually get me something special to make up for the candy, like a new video game."

"Hey, that's not a bad trade-off," said Samantha.

"I hear the arcade has some great games," said Paul.

"That's right," said Georgie. "Samantha and I go there all the time."

"Mr. Blank, the owner, sells games, too," added Samantha. "He's got all the latest ones. And good prices."

Just then the school bell rang.

"Aww," sighed Mortimer. "Lunch is over."

"See you later, guys," said Paul.

"Maybe we'll see you at the arcade this weekend," said Samantha.

"Yeah, that would be great," Paul said.

That Saturday, the Clue Club had their weekly meeting at Polly's house.

"There's a new mystery video game out called *I Haven't Got a Clue*," said Samantha. "I saw it at the arcade yesterday."

"Let's check it out after our meeting," said Georgie.

"I don't know," said Mortimer. "Video games bore me."

"I'm with you, Mortimer," said Polly.

"Me, three," agreed Wendy.

"Hey," said Peter. "I'll give anything a chance if it has the word 'Clue' in its name."

"I guess I'll come," said Mortimer. "If I don't like it, I can always play a game of pinball."

"That's true," said Polly. "You coming, Wendy?"

"Sure," agreed Wendy. "Why not? We're the Clue Club. We ought to check out any new mystery game."

After a game of Clue Jr., the six friends headed over to the arcade. Standing in front of the new mystery game was Paul Pearly.

"Hey, Paul," called Georgie. "How's the new game?"

"It's the best video game I've ever played," said Paul. "I've been here for an hour."

"How about giving us a turn?" asked Georgie.

"Okay," Paul said.

Samantha and Georgie played partners for a round, and then the others gave it a try.

"I have to admit it," said Mortimer. "This game is more fun than any video game I've ever played."

"It could change my mind about video games, too," agreed Polly.

"Me, three," said Wendy.

"I want it for my own system," said Paul.

"Halloween's a long way off," laughed Georgie.

"I can't wait that long," said Paul. "I'll have to figure something out."

The others watched as Georgie and Paul played partners. After Paul won, he and Samantha played a game. Paul won that game, too, then he and Georgie played another game.

"You're really good, Paul!" Georgie said.

"Thanks," said Paul.

"You won every game," Wendy said.

"Well, I gotta go," said Polly. "I have to be home for dinner."

"Umm, dinner," said Mortimer. "Can't be late for food."

"See you later, Paul," Samantha said.

"Okay," said Paul, who was already back at the mystery game.

*　　*　　*

The next day, Wendy called Polly early in the morning. "I never thought I'd say this, Polly, but I want to play the mystery video game!"

"You know, I was just thinking about what fun it was," said Polly. "Listen! The arcade opens in fifteen minutes. Meet you there."

When Polly and Wendy arrived, they found Samantha and Georgie waiting outside the arcade.

"I don't believe it!" said Samantha, laughing.

"Speaking of unbelievable," said Georgie. "Look who else is coming!" He pointed to Mortimer and Peter coming around the corner. "I thought you guys didn't like video games," he called out.

"But this one is different," said Mortimer, looking embarrassed.

Just then Mr. Blank opened the door to the store. "Come in, kids," he said. "Sorry

19

to open late, but it looks like I was robbed last night. I've been double-checking my stock."

When everyone was inside, Mr. Blank continued. "When I got here this morning, the door was unlocked. The lock wasn't broken, so I'll bet someone hid in the store when I closed, and then left later."

Mr. Blank walked over to the mystery arcade game and pointed to the floor in front of it.

"Just look at the mess they left behind," Mr. Blank frowned, shaking his head. "Litter all over the floor. They must have played the new mystery game for awhile last night. You kids go ahead and play. I want to finish counting my stock to see if anything is missing."

"We'll help you clean up, Mr. Blank," said Wendy.

The Clue Club kids picked up the litter, then began playing the mystery game. Soon the store was busy with kids coming in and out. Everything was peaceful until

Richie Royal, the town bully, burst through the door. He elbowed Georgie away from the mystery game.

"Hey, watch it, Richie," yelled Georgie. "I'm playing now."

"Stand aside and watch a master," sneered Richie.

"A master what?" said Samantha. "Master creep?"

"Oooh, you scare me," Richie teased. "Anyway, I'm next. I'll show you guys what a little practice can do. I'm gonna beat that Pearly wimp."

Just then, Mr. Blank came over to the kids. "I discovered what the thief took," he told them. "A copy of that new *I Haven't Got a Clue* game. You kids were playing the arcade game yesterday. Did you see anything suspicious?"

"We played it yesterday afternoon," said Polly. "With Paul Pearly."

"I didn't notice anything odd," said Peter.

"Me, either," agreed Wendy.

"Weren't you playing it, too?" Mr. Blank asked Richie.

"Yeah, but I had to leave before you closed because my mom is sick," said Richie. "That Pearly was the one playing it last night. He was here way after I left. He thinks he's so hot on the game. We're supposed to have a match today to see who's best. I bet Pearly took your game so he could practice."

"It couldn't be Paul," said Mortimer.

"Why not, Mortimer?" said Mr. Blank.

"So you haven't a clue about that missing mystery game, huh, Richie?" said Mortimer. "I think I have three clues, and they don't point to Paul."

How does Mortimer know Paul didn't steal the video game?

today. I'll go home and get it. I'll bring it right back."

"I think I'll go with you to get it, Richie," said Mr. Blank. "That way we can make sure your mother knows what happened. And we can tell her why you aren't allowed in my store anymore."

"Looks like the old saying, 'Practice Makes Perfect,' didn't work for you, Richie," said Georgie.

Solution
The Case of the Mystery Video Game

"Yeah, yeah," sighed Richie, pretending to yawn. "So what are they?"

"I know one," said Samantha. "The litter around the arcade game."

"Right," said Georgie. "There were candy wrappers, and Paul can't eat candy."

"Clue number two," said Polly. "How did Richie know the video was taken after Mr. Blank closed last night?"

"Unless he took it," said Wendy. "That way, he knew *when* it was taken."

"And clue number three," said Peter. "How did Richie know Paul was at the store for a long time after he left?"

"He couldn't," said Mortimer. "Unless he never left."

"Hmmm," said Mr. Blank. "What do you have to say about that, Richie?"

"Uhh, I was just borrowing the game, Mr. Blank," Richie stuttered. "I needed to practice it last night so I could beat Pearly

The Case of the Fishy Horoscope

Samantha Scarlet woke up before her alarm went off at five o'clock. Her uncle had given her a new fishing rod for her birthday and today she was going to use it for the first time. The Clue Club kids were going fishing off the pier at the boat marina.

At six sharp, Mortimer Mustard arrived at Samantha's house. Mortimer headed straight for the refrigerator and poured himself a glass of orange juice.

"Look, Mortimer," Samantha said, holding out the fishing rod. "Isn't it beautiful?"

"Cool!" Mortimer said. "Your uncle even got you a bait box!"

Just then the doorbell rang. It was Polly Peacock, Wendy White, and Georgie Green.

"We're here," yawned Wendy.

"I brought the bait," said Georgie. "Look. Some nice juicy worms."

"Yuk!" cried Polly. "I use fake lures."

"Guess who's late," said Samantha.

"Peter, of course," said Wendy.

"He'd better hurry or we won't get a good spot at the pier," said Mortimer, chewing on a doughnut.

"Here I am!" called Peter, running down the street. "Where's your new fishing rod?"

"Come on," Samantha said. "I'll show you my new pole at the pier. I might even let you use it."

The kids chased each other out the back door, hopped on their bikes, and rode off to the marina. When they were parking their bikes, they saw Tony Twotone and Ben Beige in front of the marina office. Tony and Ben were two sixth-grade boys from their school. As the Clue Club came closer, they saw that Tony and Ben were having an argument with Ms. Skipper, the manager of the marina.

"Hi, guys," called Mortimer. "What's up?"

"Hey, Mort," said Tony. "Ms. Skipper thinks we took one of her rowboats out fishing last night."

"Mr. and Mrs. Rudder told me they saw two boys bringing a boat in around nine o'clock," Ms. Skipper told them. "They ran off before the Rudders could catch them. Both boys were your size, thin and not very tall."

"I'm not short!" said Ben angrily.

"You're short for your age, Ben," said Mortimer. "Hey, don't worry about it. You'll get a growth spurt."

"Whatever," interrupted Tony. "There are lots of boys our size, Ms. Skipper. Why do you think it was us?"

"The Rudders said the boys were also wearing jean jackets with Shark emblems on the back, just like yours," Ms. Skipper added.

"But other *short* kids have Shark emblems on the backs of their jean jackets," retorted Ben. "That doesn't prove anything."

"That's true, but I also found Tony's tackle box in the boat this morning," said Ms. Skipper.

"Oh, yeah," said Tony. "I was coming to tell you I left it on the dock yesterday. Whoever took the boat must have taken my tackle box, too."

"I find that a little hard to believe, Tony," said Ms. Skipper. "I think you had to leave it behind when the Rudders chased you. Don't you know it's dangerous to take a boat out at night? Not to mention against the law."

"We weren't around the marina last night," said Tony. "We were at the mall."

"What's the problem anyway?" said Ben. "The boat is okay. Nobody stole it or smashed it up or anything."

"What's the problem?" Ms. Skipper said angrily. "What's wrong with you boys? What if the boat had tipped over? What if you had fallen into the water? You could have drowned out on the river at night."

"No one can have any fun anymore. You have to make sure you're S-A-F-E," said Ben in a singsong voice.

"Shut up, Ben!" said Tony. "It doesn't have anything to do with us, anyway. We weren't here. We were at the mall."

"I'm sorry, boys, but I think you were here," insisted Ms. Skipper.

"We were at the mall and I can prove it," declared Ben. "There's a machine in one of the stores that tells your horoscope. It prints the date and the time and your horoscope on a card. Look, here's mine."

"Uhh . . . I lost mine," said Tony. "But I was with Ben all night."

"Is it true about the horoscope machine?" Ms. Skipper asked the Clue Club kids.

"That's right," said Samantha. "It's in the candy store. I think it's called *Have a Good Day.*"

"It's cool," said Georgie. "You stand on this scale and put in a dime. Then you punch in your birthday and the machine prints out your horoscope on a card."

"All right, Ben," Ms. Skipper said. "Let's see the card." Ben handed Ms. Skipper his horoscope card. It read:

HAVE A GOOD DAY HOROSCOPE
FRIDAY, APRIL 3, 8:30 P.M.
YOUR BIRTHDAY: OCTOBER 5
YOUR WEIGHT: 186 POUNDS
YOUR HOROSCOPE:
TOMORROW YOU WILL GET
A BIG SURPRISE

"Well, this horoscope card certainly has last night's date on it," Ms. Skipper said. "And the time says eight-thirty. The Rudders saw the boys bring the rowboat back at nine o'clock. That means the boat was taken out before nine. If you were in the mall at eight-thirty, you couldn't have been here at the same time. I guess I made a mistake." She started to hand Ben his card

but dropped it. "Whoops," she said. "Sorry."

"I've got it, Ms. Skipper," said Peter, bending down to pick up the card. As he straightened up, he looked at it. "Wait a minute," he said. "Take a look at this, guys."

"Why don't you keep out of this, Peter?" Ben said. "Give me the card."

Peter handed the card to Wendy. After she read it, she passed it to the rest of the Clue kids. "I see what you mean, Peter," she said.

"I do, too," said Polly. "I thought their story sounded fishy."

"Maybe you two did take the boat out, after all," said Peter. "It sure looks like you were lying about where you were last night."

Why does Peter think Ben and Tony are lying about being at the mall?

per. "I'm going to have to ban you from the marina until you can be more responsible."

"I told you using your dad's horoscope wouldn't work," Tony told Ben.

"Yep, your horoscope story didn't carry much weight," said Georgie. "Well, actually," he added, laughing, "it had too much weight!"

Solution
The Case of the Fishy Horoscope

"What do you mean, we're lying?" shouted Ben. "There's our proof. The horoscope card has last night's date on it."

"Yes, it does, but it's not your card," said Peter.

"What do you mean?" asked Ms. Skipper.

"I weigh about ninety pounds and Ben is not that much taller than me," said Georgie.

"Look at the weight on the card," said Wendy. "It says one hundred eighty-six pounds!"

"So you were lying about being at the mall last night," said Ms. Skipper.

"I'll bet I know why," said Samantha. "Because you were out on the boat."

"So what?" Ben said. "What difference does it make? Nothing bad happened to the boat. We didn't drown."

"No, but you could have," said Ms. Skip-

The Case of the Famous Artist

The Clue Club was finishing up their weekly meeting and making plans for the weekend. Peter Plum looked out the window. It had been raining all day. "Why don't we bike over to Flannel Field tomorrow?" he said. "It's supposed to stop raining this evening, and tomorrow's going to be nice and sunny."

"If we leave early in the morning we can spend the day there," said Polly Peacock. "We can have a picnic and play Clue Jr."

The kids decided that each one of them would bring something special to eat. They would meet at Peter's house at nine. Then they would ride their bicycles to Flannel Field together.

"What's that big notebook you're taking?" Georgie Green asked Wendy White when she rode up to Peter's house the next morning.

"It's an artist's pad," Wendy answered. "And my watercolors are in my backpack."

"I didn't know you were an artist!" Mortimer Mustard said.

"I like to paint flowers," Wendy said. "I figure there will be plenty of them to paint today."

The kids headed out to Flannel Field. "This is a MOST EXCELLENT day," Samantha Scarlet shouted. She was way ahead of the others on her bike.

The road to Flannel Field passed by the Pinetree Lumberyard. Suddenly Samantha yelled, "Stop! Look at that!" She pointed to the lumberyard warehouse on the left side of the road.

"Wow!" said Peter. The side of the warehouse was covered with brightly colored graffiti designs. In one corner it was signed, BY A FAMOUS ARTIST.

"I wonder who did that?" whispered Polly.

"Boy, whoever did it is going to be in trouble," Mortimer said.

"I guess that's one way to become a famous artist," said Georgie.

"Look," Wendy said. "By the gate. There's Mr. Wood, the watchman." The kids leaned their bikes against the fence that went around the lumberyard and ran to the gate.

"Can we take a look at the graffiti, Mr. Wood?" Samantha asked.

"Sure, you can look at it," Mr. Wood said. "It's hard to miss! This is a good example of how *not* to express yourself," he said. "What a mess."

"Looks like the famous artist got messy, too," said Mortimer. He pointed to some footprints in the mud around the warehouse.

"Hmm," said Peter. "Look at the star design in these footprints. The famous artist was wearing sneakers."

"You're not the only ones who wanted to look at this graffiti," said Mr. Wood. "A bunch of kids are here — on the other side of the warehouse." The Clue kids looked around the corner of the building. There was a group of kids talking to Officer Lawford.

"They're from our school," said Georgie. "Maybe they know something."

The Clue Club walked over to join the group.

"Come on over," Officer Lawford called out, waving to them. "How come you're here?" he asked them.

"We saw the warehouse from the road and decided to take a look," said Georgie.

"Why were you on the road?" the policeman asked.

"We were riding by on our way to Flannel Field," said Samantha. "We're going to have a picnic there this morning."

Officer Lawford turned to Ralph Rust, a seventh-grader. "So you say you were at home last night, right?" he asked.

"Yeah," Ralph answered. "At my little sister's birthday party."

"Why are you here this morning?" the policeman asked him. "It's a long way from town."

"I came out to ride my mountain bike in the woods," said Ralph. "I stopped when I saw the graffiti."

"How about you two?" Officer Lawford said to Tammy Turquoise and Vincent Violet, two fifth-graders.

"Nora Navy came to the lumberyard with her father this morning," answered Tammy. "She called me when she got back to tell me about the graffiti."

"I live next door to Tammy," said Vincent. "She told me about it and we decided to come take a look."

"How about you, Billy?" Officer Lawford asked Billy Blond, a seventh-grader. "What were you doing here this morning?"

"I just came back to look at the graffiti," Billy said.

"How did you know about it?" Officer Lawford asked.

"I heard about it on the TV news this morning," answered Billy.

"You were here pretty early," said Mr. Wood.

"Is that a crime?" asked Billy.

"No. I just didn't think the story was out yet," said Mr. Wood.

"Well, I heard about it and I wanted to see it," said Billy.

"What station did you hear it on?" asked Mr. Wood.

"I don't remember!" Billy said.

"Where were you last night?" Officer Lawford asked.

"At the movies, where it was nice and dry," Billy answered impatiently. "I haven't been on this road since last Fourth of July. That's when I went to the fireworks show at Flannel Field. Can I go now? I have to get back to town. I'm supposed to do some chores for my dad."

"I guess so," said Officer Lawford. "I guess everyone can leave. Just give me your home phone numbers so I can speak with your parents. I need to ask them where you were last night."

Everyone started to leave. Then Billy turned around. "Oh, I almost forgot — again," he said to himself. He walked toward a backpack lying on the ground near the warehouse.

"Is this yours?" Mr. Wood said to Billy, reaching down to pick up the backpack for him. "Oh, yes. I see your name on it."

"No!" Billy shouted. He stepped between the watchman and the backpack. "I mean, yes, it's mine. I'll get it." He picked up his backpack carefully and started to leave again.

"Watch out for the mud!" cried Mr. Wood. But he was too late. Billy had stepped into the soft ground.

"That's okay," Billy said, pulling his foot up. "My sneakers are already muddy."

"Wait a minute, Billy," said Wendy. "I think you knew about the graffiti before it

came out on the TV news — if it *was* on the news."

"Well, if you know so much, Wendy, you tell me how I knew about it," said Billy.

"You knew about the graffiti because you did it," said Wendy.

"Why do you say that, Wendy?" asked Officer Lawford.

"Look at Billy's shoes," replied Wendy. "They're muddy."

"So, they're muddy," said Billy. "It's been raining."

"Yes, but you got yours muddy when you spray-painted the warehouse," said Wendy.

"You can't prove I spray-painted the graffiti just because I have muddy sneakers," Billy said.

Why does Wendy think Billy was the one who spray-painted graffiti on the warehouse?

Solution
The Case of the Famous Artist

"Your sneakers were here last night," said Wendy. "When you painted a design on the warehouse, your sneakers made one in the mud." She pointed to Billy's fresh footprint.

"Hey! That footprint has a star in it," said Polly. "It's just like the footprints on the other side of the warehouse — the side where all the graffiti was painted."

"Other kids have sneakers with stars on the bottoms," said Billy.

"Maybe. But you made one more slipup," said Wendy. "Remember why you said you were at the warehouse this morning?"

"I said I came to see the graffiti," said Billy. "Just like you."

"No, you didn't," said Peter. "You said you came *back* to look at the graffiti."

"Why would you say you came back if you were never here?" said Mortimer.

"That was a mistake!" Billy shouted. "I

didn't mean that." He turned quickly to leave. As he did, a clinking sound came from his backpack.

"Hold on," said Officer Lawford. "I think these kids might be right. Let's see what you have in your bag." When he opened the backpack, Officer Lawford found several empty cans of spray paint inside.

"You came back for this today, didn't you, son?" said Officer Lawford. "You had to, since it had your name on it."

"Okay," said Billy. "I forgot it when I spray-painted the warehouse last night."

"Now you'll have to give the warehouse another paint job," said Officer Lawford. "Only this time, it will be to cover up the graffiti."

"Well, you may not be a famous artist, Billy, but you'll be a famous painter," said Georgie.

The Case of the Small Fortune Cookies

The three grade schools in town were having a fund-raiser to help pay for new computers. A combination bake sale and flea market was being set up in the high school gym on Saturday. Everyone in town was contributing something.

Early Saturday morning, people began arriving with cakes, cookies, used clothes and toys, plants, homemade gifts, books, and even video games.

The Clue Club kids set up a Clue Jr. booth. People would pay twenty-five cents to play a game and the winner would receive fifty cents. The rest of the money would go toward the computer fund.

"Well, our tables are all set up," said Polly Peacock.

"Oh, look at all the food that's coming in," said Mortimer Mustard.

"My mom and dad were up all night baking," said Peter Plum. "They said getting computers is one of the most important things the school can do."

"Everyone in town is talking about the special cookies your mom and dad made," said Samantha Scarlet.

"Oh, yeah, the ones with money baked in them?" Peter said, smiling. "That news got around fast, didn't it?"

"And the cookies are going to go fast, too," said Mortimer.

"There's your parents' minivan now," said Georgie, looking out a window.

"Let's help carry in the food," said Wendy White.

Outside, Mr. and Mrs. Plum were handing out boxes and trays to children to carry into the gym.

"Our table is the long one in the corner," said Mr. Plum. "Next to the soda booth, under the basketball hoop."

"Hi, kids," said Mrs. Plum.

"We heard about your special cookies," said Mortimer.

"Ah, yes, our *fortune* cookies," Mrs. Plum said, smiling. "Most of them have a fortune in them. But some have a dollar bill inside."

"It's only a *small* fortune," laughed Mr. Plum, "but we figured it would be enough to make people buy them."

"Get your hot cookies, stuffed with cold cash," said Georgie Green.

"Well, I think that's everything," said Mrs. Plum. "Why don't you park the van and I'll meet you inside, dear?"

The kids helped Mrs. Plum arrange her baked goods on the table. "This is so odd," she said. "I don't see those fortune cookies anywhere." Just then her husband walked in. "Who carried in the fortune cookies?" she asked him.

"That boy over there, in the striped T-shirt." Mr. Plum pointed to the boy running the soda booth.

"That's Jim Brownsville, Dad," said Peter.

"Would you find out where he put them?" asked Mrs. Plum.

Mr. Plum and the kids went over to the soda booth. "Hi, Jim," said Mr. Plum.

"Hello, sir," Jim answered.

"Where did you put the box of cookies you carried in from my van, Jim?" Mr. Plum asked.

"I put them on your table," Jim said with a smile.

"Hmmm. The whole box seems to have disappeared," Mr. Plum said.

Jim's smile faded. "Well, I don't know anything about that," he said. "Ask Frank Bluer if you don't believe me." He pointed to a boy in the hot dog booth nearby.

Jim waved at Frank. "Come here a second," he called. Frank ran over to the soda booth.

"Frank," said Jim. "Did you see me bring in a box of cookies from the Plums' minivan a little while ago?"

"Sure," Frank replied. "You set the box of cookies down on the table and went straight to the soda booth."

"Are you sure you saw him put it on the right table?" asked Mr. Plum.

"Oh, yeah," said Frank. "I was putting the hot dog buns in the steamer when he walked by."

"You didn't notice anyone else picking up that box, did you?" asked Mrs. Plum.

"Nope," said Frank.

"Well, this is a mystery," said Mr. Plum.

"That's a drag, Dad. Those were really going to sell," said Peter.

"Maybe they'll turn up," said Samantha.

By nine o'clock all the booths were set up and ready for the crowds outside. As soon as the doors opened, the gym was jammed. Kids from all over town kept the three Clue Jr. game boards full.

Around lunchtime, Mortimer said, "I've been smelling those hot dogs all morning. I'm going to have one for lunch."

"Me, too," said Georgie.

"Me, three," said Wendy.

"Maybe I'll have three, too," Peter said.

"Why don't we let someone take over the booth for a couple of minutes?" suggested Polly. "Then we can all go have a hot dog."

"Polly, what a hot idea," said Samantha.

Peter rounded up a couple of kids to watch the booth, and all six Clue Club kids lined up at the hot dog stand. Jim Brownsville from the soda booth walked up and stood behind them.

The kids talked about the new computers their schools would be getting. Soon Mortimer was at the head of the line.

"I'll have two," Mortimer told Frank. Frank turned around and grabbed two hot dog buns from the steamer. Turning back, he forked the hot dogs from a pot of hot water and placed them in the buns.

"What do you want on them?" he asked Mortimer.

"Oh, mustard and sauerkraut," Mortimer answered.

"I want everything on mine," Georgie said.

Frank turned for the bun and speared a hot dog for Georgie.

"I guess you *all* need sodas now, right?" Jim asked from the next booth.

"First, I think we need that box of fortune cookies you took, Jim," said Georgie.

"Cookies? Oh, no," said Jim. "I thought we got that straight."

"No, you just thought you and Frank got your stories straight," said Georgie.

"Me?" exclaimed Frank. "What are you talking about?"

"I think you both took Mr. and Mrs. Plum's cookies," said Georgie.

Why does Georgie think Jim and Frank took the cookies?

Solution
The Case of the Small Fortune Cookies

"Me?" protested Frank. "Jim brought them inside. I saw him."

"No, you didn't," said Georgie. "You're lying and the hot dog bun steamer gave you away."

"You guys have been playing too many mystery games," said Frank, shaking his head. "The hot dog bun steamer gave me away?"

"Right," said Mortimer. "You have to turn around to take the buns out of the steamer."

"So?" said Frank.

"So. When you did that, your back was to us," said Samantha.

"You said you were putting buns into the steamer when Jim brought the cookies in," said Wendy.

"But if you were, you couldn't have seen him walk by the front of your booth," said Mortimer.

"Or put the cookies on the Plums' table," said Polly.

"That means you both took the cookies and gave each other alibis," said Georgie.

Peter called his parents over to the hot dog stand and explained what had just happened.

"Boys," Mr. Plum said. "Should we check through your things?"

"No," said Frank, hanging his head. "Here are your cookies," And he handed over the box of cookies.

"Frank and Jim didn't have a very good fortune today, did they?" said Wendy.

"No," said Georgie. "Their fortune should read, *Beware of the Dogs* — hot dogs, that is."

The Case of the Missing Monkey

"**M**ortimer, Polly is on the phone," Mr. Mustard called upstairs.

Mortimer Mustard ran down and picked up the phone. "Hello?"

"Peter Plum just called me with some bad news about Georgie," Polly Peacock said. "Georgie's monkey, Bingo, is missing. Georgie wants us to help him put up signs in the neighborhood. He's pretty upset."

"I'll call the others and meet you at his house," said Mortimer. Quickly Mortimer called Samantha Scarlet and Wendy White. In fifteen minutes, the Clue Club kids were all at Georgie Green's house. Georgie was waiting for them outside in the front yard. He was wearing paint-splattered clothes and looking very sad.

"Don't walk on the front porch steps,"

Georgie told everyone. "Dad and I just painted them this morning."

"So what happened to Bingo?" asked Samantha.

"I let him out with Dad and me while we were painting the porch steps," Georgie began. "After we finished painting, we carried the paint back to the garage. When I came back around the front, Bingo was gone!"

"Did you call the police?" asked Peter.

"Right away," answered Georgie.

"Gosh, it's not like Bingo to run off," said Samantha.

"No," agreed Wendy. "Not like Petunia. That parrot of mine loves to fly away."

"I know," wailed Georgie. "That's why I'm really worried."

"Suppose someone kidnapped him?" said Polly. "Monkeys aren't your average pets, you know. Not like a turtle. No one would take my Speedo."

"I know how you feel, Georgie," said

Peter, thinking about his dog. "I sure would worry if Bizzy ran off."

"Well, it's not doing any good to sit around and worry," said Mortimer impatiently. "We'd better put up some signs!"

"We have to use the side steps," said Georgie. "The front steps won't be dry for a day or so."

The kids ran around to the side of the porch to a staircase behind some bushes. They dashed up the steps and across the porch. Everyone was eager to help find Bingo.

"I've got paper and stuff on the dining room table," said Georgie. "We can work in there."

"I brought some of my Day-Glo markers," said Wendy. "Bright colors will catch people's attention."

"Mom and Dad said I can offer a reward, too," said Georgie. "Fifty dollars!"

The kids made up a stack of signs with Georgie's phone number.

"Make the reward part big," Georgie reminded the others. "I want to make sure people see it."

"And use the red marker to write it," said Wendy.

When the signs were finished, the kids stuck them up all over town. They put them up at the school, on telephone poles and neighborhood fences, inside the bank, the post office, stores — everywhere! Finally, around dinnertime, they headed back to Georgie's house.

"Thanks, guys," Georgie told his friends. "I feel a little better. At least the whole town now knows Bingo is missing."

"Yeah," said Samantha. "I'm sure someone will spot him."

"You'll have him back in no time," said Polly, patting Georgie's shoulder. "Don't worry."

"Call us if anything happens," said Peter.

*　　*　　*

Later that evening, Peter got a phone call from Georgie. "Guess what?" Georgie shouted. "Some kid named Steve Yellowstone found Bingo! He's bringing him over to the house at seven o'clock. Call everybody and tell them to come over. Mom says we'll all go out for ice cream to celebrate."

"Hey! I guess the signs worked," said Peter. "That's great, Georgie. I'll call the others."

At six-thirty, the Clue Club kids were gathered at Georgie's house. Georgie was so excited he couldn't sit still. "Let's all go outside on the porch and watch for Bingo," he told the others.

Everyone sat on the edge of their chairs. For a while Georgie paced back and forth across the porch. Finally, he sat down, too. A little after seven o'clock, a teenage boy walked up to the house. "Are you Georgie?" he asked.

"Yeah!" cried Georgie, leaping to his feet. "Are you Steve Yellowstone?"

"That's me," the boy answered.

"Do you have Bingo?" Georgie said.

"He's in the car," said the boy. "I'll bring him."

Steve went to his car where he had Bingo in the backseat. Coming across the yard, he bounded up the side steps and handed Bingo to Georgie.

"Here's your missing monkey," Steve said.

"Bingo, you bad monkey," scolded Georgie, hugging his pet and scratching him on the head.

"I'm so glad Bingo's home," sighed Polly.

"Ahh, your signs said something about a reward," said Steve.

"Oh, yeah, come on in," said Georgie.

Inside the house, Mr. Green asked Steve, "Where did you find Bingo?"

"Uhhh, I found him hanging around a couple of blocks away," Steve said. "You know, I gotta get back home. Maybe we could settle up this reward thing."

"I'll bet he was in the park, Steve, right?" Samantha asked.

"Hey, that's right," Steve said, smiling. "He was sitting on a swing."

"I don't think Steve found Bingo at all," said Samantha.

"What do you mean?" asked Steve. "How did I get him if I didn't find him?"

"You got him lost before you found him," stated Samantha. "Mr. Green, maybe we should call the police."

"Call the police? What's wrong with you, Samantha?" shouted Georgie. "Steve found Bingo. Bingo's safe because of him!"

"Bingo was safe before Steve found him," said Samantha. "Steve stole Bingo."

Why does Samantha think Steve stole Bingo?

Georgie yelled at Steve, "You took Bingo while Dad and I were in the garage. You kidnapped Bingo!"

"I just wanted a neat pet," said Steve. "I would have taken good care of him. But then I saw the signs. I figured I could buy my own monkey with the reward."

"You should have tried to *earn* some money to buy a pet, young man," said Mr. Green. "I'm afraid we will have to call the police now."

"Looks like you painted yourself into a corner, Steve," said Polly.

Solution
The Case of the Missing Monkey

"Let's all calm down," said Mr. Green. "It's been a difficult day. Samantha, maybe you should tell us why you think Steve took Bingo."

"Because of the way he stepped up to return him," said Samantha.

Everyone sat there for a moment. Then Mortimer jumped up. "I get it!" he shouted. "The steps. Steve came up the side steps."

"Hey, no one told you to come up the side steps," Georgie said to Steve.

"That's right," said Polly. "You can hardly see those steps even in the daytime, let alone at night."

"Steve knew to use them," cried Wendy. "He must have known the front steps had wet paint on them."

"There's only one way he could have known that," said Peter. "He saw Georgie and Mr. Green painting them."

The Case of the Musical Racket

The first thing Polly Peacock did when she came home from her violin lesson was call Peter Plum. "I can't go to the next Clue Club meeting," she told him.

"Why? What's wrong?" Peter asked.

"I have a violin recital Sunday," Polly said.

"Clue meeting is on Saturday, Polly," Peter said.

"Well, tomorrow and the next day, all the players are going to the music school for a run-through," Polly said.

"Everyone is here at my house," Peter told her. "My mom made a new kind of brownies and she's trying them out on everybody. Head on over and we can all decide what to do together."

"Great, Peter," said Polly. "I'll be right there. Save me some brownies."

"Polly's rehearsal is pretty important," said Wendy White. "Why don't we just have our Clue Jr. meeting afterward?"

"I know! Let's have the meeting at Mama Sophie's Pizza Parlor," suggested Georgie Green.

"An excellent suggestion," Mortimer Mustard piped up. "Clue Jr. and pizza go great together."

"We can meet Polly at the music school and go from there," said Samantha Scarlet.

"No more problems," said Mortimer, "unless there are no more brownies."

"I'll take one more, too," said Samantha.

"Me, three," agreed Wendy.

"Looks like there's no problem with your mom's new brownie recipe, either," Georgie told Peter.

The next morning, the Clue kids gathered in front of the music school. Then they decided to wait for Polly in the school lobby. Inside was Gwen Garnet, holding her cello case and talking to her best friend, Theresa Teal.

"Hi, Polly," Gwen said when Polly came out of her lesson room. "Ready for the big concert?"

"I guess I'm pretty excited, Gwen," Polly admitted. "I'm glad we had this last rehearsal, aren't you?"

"Definitely," agreed Gwen.

"Don't worry, you'll be great, Polly," said Peter. The Clue kids all clapped while Polly bowed.

"We're supposed to dress up," said Gwen. "I just got a new skirt to wear."

"The one you have on?" asked Samantha.

"Oh, no," laughed Gwen. "You can't play the cello in this kind of skirt. You need a full skirt so you can fit the cello between your knees."

"Come on, let's go get a pizza," Polly said.

"I'll play second fiddle to that suggestion," said Mortimer.

"Whatever," said Georgie, shaking his head at Mortimer's bad joke.

"Well, we're heading to the pizza parlor," Polly said to Gwen. "Do you want to go for some pizza with us?"

"Maybe later," said Gwen. "But I've got to go home and get rid of this cello. It's too heavy to carry around for long."

"I guess so," said Polly. "A violin is a lot easier to deal with."

The kids headed out the door and down the stairs. On the street, Mr. Blueville, owner of the sporting goods store next door, was talking with Officer Lawford.

"See you at the recital," Polly said.

"Right," said Gwen. She and Theresa started to walk off.

"Wait! There she is!" Mr. Blueville cried, pointing to Theresa. Theresa and Gwen turned around. "You walked out with that tennis racket," Mr. Blueville said to Theresa.

"What?" said Theresa. "What tennis racket?"

"The tennis racket you were looking at a little while ago in the store," Mr. Blueville said angrily. "You've been in here looking at that racket all week. Today you came in and gave it some test swings. The next thing I knew, the tennis racket was gone."

"Were you in the store this morning?" said Officer Lawford.

"Yes," said Theresa. "I was waiting for Gwen to finish her rehearsal at the music school. I got here early, so I just went into the sports store until she was ready. But I don't have any tennis racket. Where would I put it?"

"Well, Phil, she has a point," said Officer Lawford. "There's certainly no way she could hide a tennis racket on her, even in her bookbag. The racket's too big. Maybe someone else took it."

Polly leaned forward. "I think Theresa did take it, Mr. Blueville. But she had help."

Why does Polly think Theresa took the tennis racket? And who helped her?

Solution
The Case of the Musical Racket

"Why do you say Theresa had help taking the tennis racket?" asked Mr. Blueville. "She was alone in the store."

"Gwen was her accomplice," said Polly.

"Polly!" exclaimed Gwen. "Why do you say that?"

"What are you doing here today, anyway?" said Polly.

"I had a rehearsal for the recital," explained Gwen. "Just like you."

"Wrong," said Polly.

"You're right, Polly," said Wendy. "Gwen couldn't have a lesson today."

"That's ridiculous," said Gwen angrily. "How would you know when I have a lesson, Wendy?"

"I know, too," said Peter. "Because of your skirt."

"You said it yourself, Gwen," Mortimer reminded her. "You can't play the cello in that kind of skirt."

"You said you need a fuller one," said Georgie.

"So why would you be here, carrying your cello case if you didn't have a lesson?" asked Samantha.

"Maybe you came to help Theresa hide the tennis racket," said Polly.

"Let's just look inside that case," said Mr. Blueville. Sure enough, the tennis racket was inside.

"Come on, girls, we'll have to call your parents," said Officer Lawford.

"Looks like this was an open-and-shut case," laughed Georgie.

The Case of the Poster Painter

"It's a masterpiece," announced Mortimer Mustard. He stood back to admire a poster he had just finished making. "It's a first-prize poster, all right."

National Children's Book Week was coming up, and to celebrate, the library was sponsoring a poster contest. The winning poster would be photographed for a national contest.

All the Clue Club kids had entered the contest. Mortimer's parents were letting them use their basement to work on the posters. For several days, the kids had been cutting and pasting, drawing and painting after school. Today the posters had to be delivered to the library by ten o'clock for judging. Ms. Whitehouse, the head librarian, had set up the children's

75

room to display the posters for the judges.

"Are you guys finished?" asked Peter Plum.

"Mine was ready yesterday," answered Wendy White.

"I guess I'm done," said Polly Peacock. She kept dabbing at her poster with a paintbrush.

"You'll never be finished, Polly," laughed Samantha Scarlet. "Everything you do has to be perfect."

"Let us look at it, Polly," said Georgie Green. "We'll tell you if you're finished or not."

"Oh, all right," said Polly, making a face. The kids placed their posters side by side on Mortimer's Ping-Pong table.

"Yours is great, Polly," said Peter.

"Except for that one tiny little smear in the corner," said Georgie. "But no one will notice it."

"Where?" cried Polly.

"Just kidding," giggled Georgie.

"Stop, Georgie," scolded Wendy. "This isn't the time for jokes."

"We'd better get going," said Samantha. "We're supposed to have our posters at the library by ten."

"I'll tell my dad we're ready for him to take us," said Mortimer.

"We need some plastic bags to wrap our posters in," Wendy said.

"Yeah, I don't want my poster ruined because of the snow," Polly said.

In spite of the plastic bag Mortimer wrapped his poster in, he found some wet blotches on it when he got to the library. "It doesn't matter," he told the others. "I brought my paints with me just in case this happened."

"Oh, good. Let me use your blue," said Polly. "One corner of my poster got smeared."

"See, Georgie?" said Samantha, shaking her head. "You shouldn't have said anything about a smear."

The six friends hurried downstairs to the children's room to fix their posters.

After Polly and Mortimer finished touching up their posters, the kids decided to go to the Sandwich Shop for lunch.

"Good idea," agreed Mortimer.

"We can come back this afternoon, to see who won the prize," said Georgie.

"I'd have a hard time choosing," said Wendy, looking at all the posters lined up on the walls and tables.

"Yeah, there are a lot of good ones," agreed Samantha.

"Look at Sylvia Silver's," said Peter. "It's really clever."

Sylvia's poster was titled *There's No Time Like the Past, the Present, and the Future for a Book*. It showed a girl walking through space with an astronaut and a dinosaur. Each of them was holding a book. The dinosaur's book title was *My Life as a Fossil;* the girl's was *A Modern Day Gal,* and the astronaut's was *My Journey Into the Future*.

"That's a good idea," said Wendy. "She used a dinosaur to represent the past and an astronaut for the future. And the girl represents the present."

"Well, I say it's past time for lunch," said Mortimer. "I don't want to wait for the future to eat."

"You're right, Mortimer," laughed Georgie. "I say there's no *time* like the present for a sandwich."

"So let's waste no *time* getting there," giggled Wendy.

"*Sssshhhh!*" whispered one of the librarians. "Quiet, please."

The kids hurried upstairs and out of the library, trying not to laugh. All during lunch they tried to come up with more jokes about the word "time." They were having so much fun they almost missed getting back to the library before it closed.

The winners were posted at the checkout desk. First prize went to Sylvia Silver's poster. Mortimer's poster won second place, and Ida Indigo came in third.

"Hey, Mortimer, you won second prize!" exclaimed Samantha. "Congratulations."

"I told you it was a masterpiece." Mortimer smiled.

"I guess those touch-ups you did made a difference," said Peter.

"That reminds me. I left my paints just outside the children's room," Mortimer said. "I'd better get them quick."

"We'll wait for you here," said Wendy.

After Mortimer left the room, Ida Indigo came up the stairway.

"Ida!" said Samantha, running up to her. "You're a winner. Aren't you so happy?"

Ida didn't seem too excited. "Yeah, I guess so," she answered. "Third prize is better than nothing, I guess. But I really wanted to win first place."

"You did great!" said Georgie.

"Yeah, but I wanted to go to the national contest," said Ida. "Oh, well, maybe next year."

"I'm ready," said Mortimer as he came

back into the room. "Looks like someone else used my paints." He frowned. "They sure did a sloppy job of closing them up."

Ms. Whitehouse called up to the children. "It's about time to close, children. I'm just shutting off the lights." Then the children heard her cry out in surprise. "Oh! This is awful!"

The kids ran down the stairs and into the children's room, where Ms. Whitehouse was standing. "Sylvia's winning poster is ruined," she said, pointing. "Someone has globbed paint on it." She scowled down at Mortimer's plastic bag of sloppy paint jars. "And it looks like that someone might have been you, Mortimer."

"No, it wasn't me," said Mortimer. "I left my paints outside the room and just came back to get them."

"Right, Mortimer," said Ida. "You were jealous."

"Did you see anything, Ida?" asked Ms. Whitehouse.

"No," said Ida. "I just got here. I came by to see who won. Then I went downstairs to check out a book I need for a school report. Just before I came up, I saw Mortimer right outside the children's room. He had his paints."

"Mortimer, I'm surprised," Ms. Whitehouse said, before Mortimer could say anything. "If this is true, we'll have to disqualify you from the contest. Of course, we can't photograph poor Sylvia's poster. I don't know what we'll do now. It's too late to have the judges come back. I'll have to speak to the poster committee."

"Wow, maybe I'll win first prize after all," Ida said.

"Well, you wanted to win," said Polly.

"The library is closing," Ms. Whitehouse continued. "I'll have to speak with your parents this evening, Mortimer. Let's all go home. What a terrible day this has been. First the awful weather, and now this."

Everyone started walking toward the

door. "Where's your coat, Ida?" asked Ms. Whitehouse.

"Oh, right," Ida said. She started back into the library, and then stopped. "Oh, never mind. I don't need it."

"Don't need it?" exclaimed Ms. Whitehouse. "In this weather? Nonsense! Are you afraid to go downstairs by yourself? Georgie will go with you, won't you, dear?"

"Sure," said Georgie, heading for the stairwell. "I'll get it for you, Ida."

"No!" said Ida. "I forgot. I didn't wear a coat."

"Didn't wear a coat in a snowstorm?" said Ms. Whitehouse.

"I didn't need one. My mom dropped me off," said Ida. "She's going to pick me up, too."

"I'll bet you did wear a coat," said Peter.

"I just told you, Peter. I didn't wear one," said Ida.

"No. You just don't want to go get it," said Peter.

"If you get your coat, you won't win," Peter explained.

Why does Peter think Ida doesn't want to get her coat?

just wanted to win. I've never won anything."

"Well, I hope you've learned that this is not the way to win, Ida," said Ms. Whitehouse.

"And you used my paints, so I would be disqualified!" exclaimed Mortimer.

"I've heard of killing two birds with one stone, but this is killing two posters with one paintbrush," said Georgie.

Solution
The Case of the Poster Painter

"I don't understand," said Ida. "Win what?"

"The poster contest," said Peter.

"I did win third prize," said Ida.

"But you wanted to win first prize so you could go to the national contest," said Peter.

"Are you saying Ida ruined Sylvia's poster so she could win the contest, Peter?" Ms. Whitehouse asked. "If you are, you'd better have some proof."

"My proof is her coat," said Peter.

"I think I know why Ida doesn't want to get her coat," said Wendy. "Her coat is in the children's room."

"She went into the children's room," said Samantha. "And there's only one reason why she would lie about it."

"Because she's the one who put paint on Sylvia's poster," said Polly.

"You won't understand," Ida said. "I

Pony Pals

Do you love ponies?

Be a Pony Pal®!

Anna, Pam, and Lulu want you to join them on adventures with their favorite ponies!

Order now and you get a free pony portrait bookmark and two collecting cards in all the books—for you *and* your pony pal!

☐ BBC48583-0	#1 I Want a Pony	$2.99
☐ BBC48584-9	#2 A Pony for Keeps	$2.99
☐ BBC48585-7	#3 A Pony in Trouble	$2.99
☐ BBC48586-5	#4 Give Me Back My Pony	$2.99
☐ BBC25244-5	#5 Pony to the Rescue	$2.99
☐ BBC25245-3	#6 Too Many Ponies	$2.99
☐ BBC54338-5	#7 Runaway Pony	$2.99
☐ BBC54339-3	#8 Good-bye Pony	$2.99
☐ BBC62974-3	#9 The Wild Pony	$2.99
☐ BBC62975-1	#10 Don't Hurt My Pony	$2.99
☐ BBC86597-8	#11 Circus Pony	$2.99
☐ BBC86598-6	#12 Keep Out, Pony!	$2.99
☐ BBC86600-1	#13 The Girl Who Hated Ponies	$2.99
☐ BBC86601-X	#14 Pony-Sitters	$3.50
☐ BBC86632-X	#15 The Blind Pony	$3.50
☐ BBC74210-8	Pony Pals Super Special #1:The Baby Pony	$5.99

Available wherever you buy books, or use this order form.

LITTLE 🍎 APPLE®

Here are some of our favorite Little Apples.

Once you take a bite out of a Little Apple book—you'll want to read more!

Books for Kids with BIG Appetites!